Sassy and Callie (her dog) and a Wagon Full of What-Ifs

ISBN 978-1-0980-4687-3 (paperback)
ISBN 978-1-64515-389-4 (hardcover)
ISBN 978-1-64515-388-7 (digital)

Copyright © 2020 by Nicole O'Brien

All rights reserved. No part of this publication may be reproduced, distributed, or transmitted in any form or by any means, including photocopying, recording, or other electronic or mechanical methods without the prior written permission of the publisher. For permission requests, solicit the publisher via the address below.

Christian Faith Publishing, Inc.
832 Park Avenue
Meadville, PA 16335
www.christianfaithpublishing.com

Printed in the United States of America

Sassy and Callie (her dog) and a Wagon Full of What-Ifs
FRUITS AND VEGGIES

A girl with a Sensational
Imagination
and a Whole Lot of
Questions!!!

By:
Nicole O'Brien
Something Sassy LLC

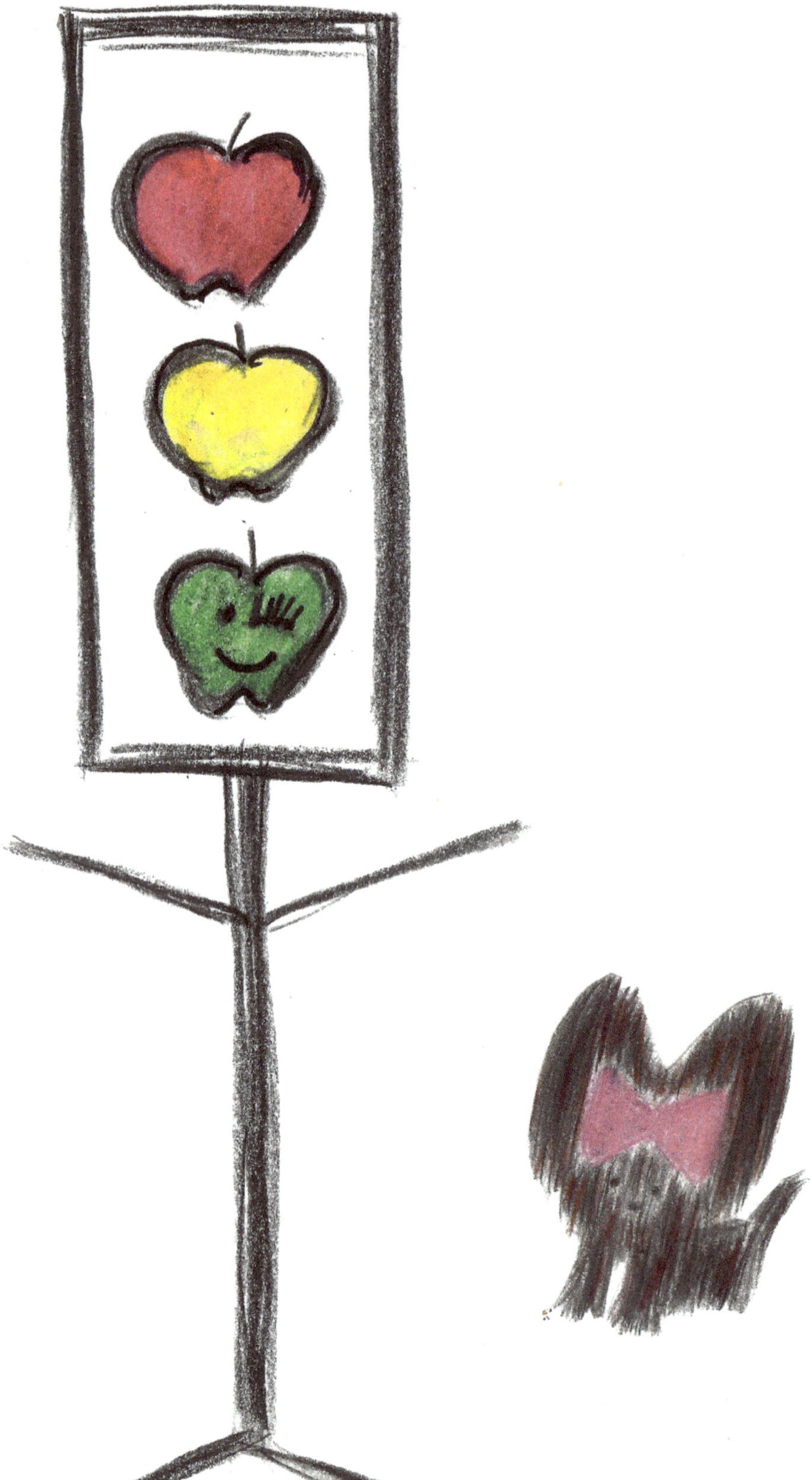

What if I only ate **APPLES**? Would my skin appear glossy and red? Would I have one little stem of hair sticking straight up on my head?

Maybe my color would change, a flash from red, yellow, to green. No doubt about it, the most delicious traffic light you have ever seen! (Woo-hoo!)

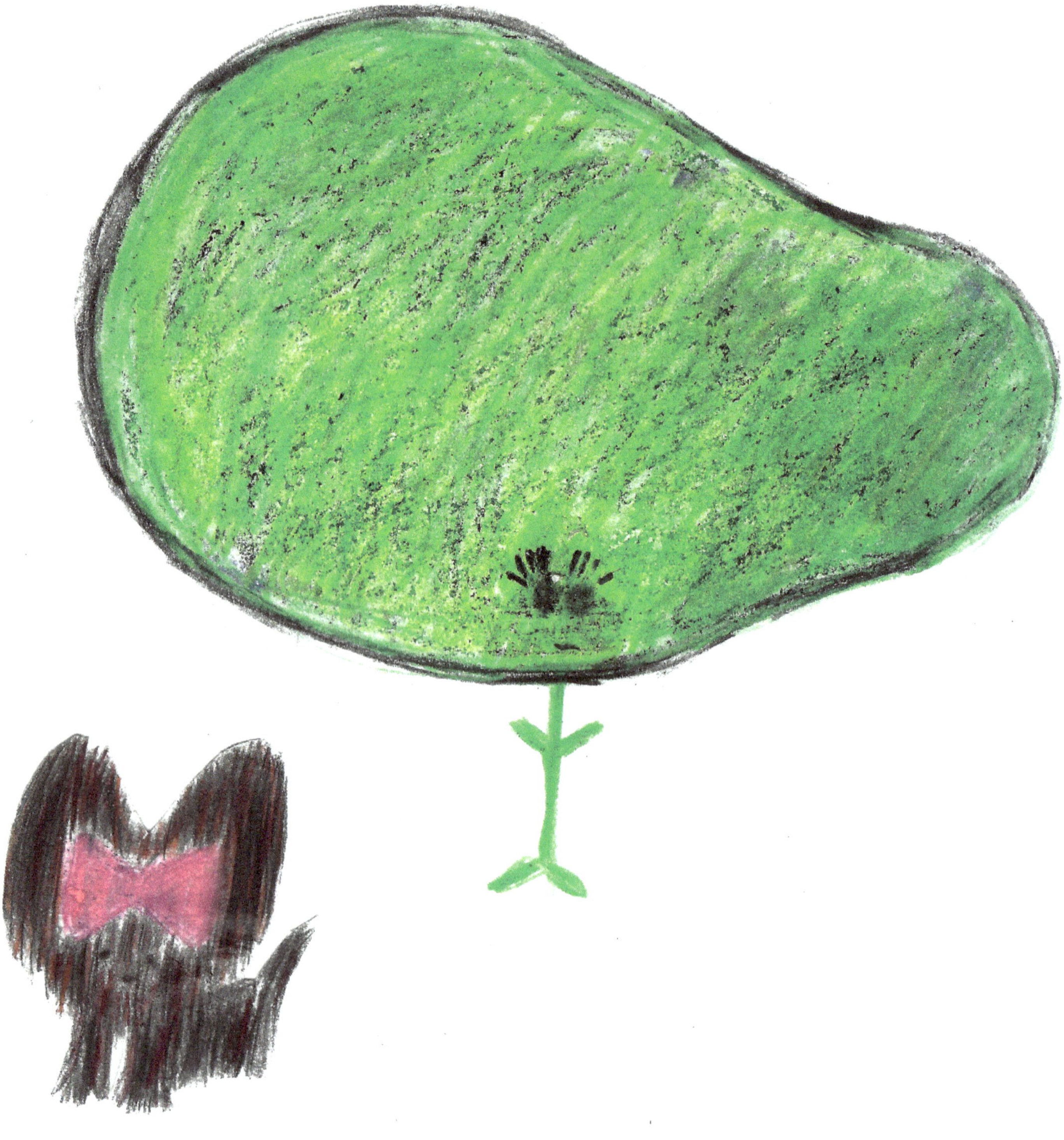

What if I only ate **AVOCADOS**? Would I turn to a deep shade of purple or a dark shade of green?

Would I be lumpy but soft like a handful of cotton, but I guess not that soft because that means I'm rotten! (Not me!)

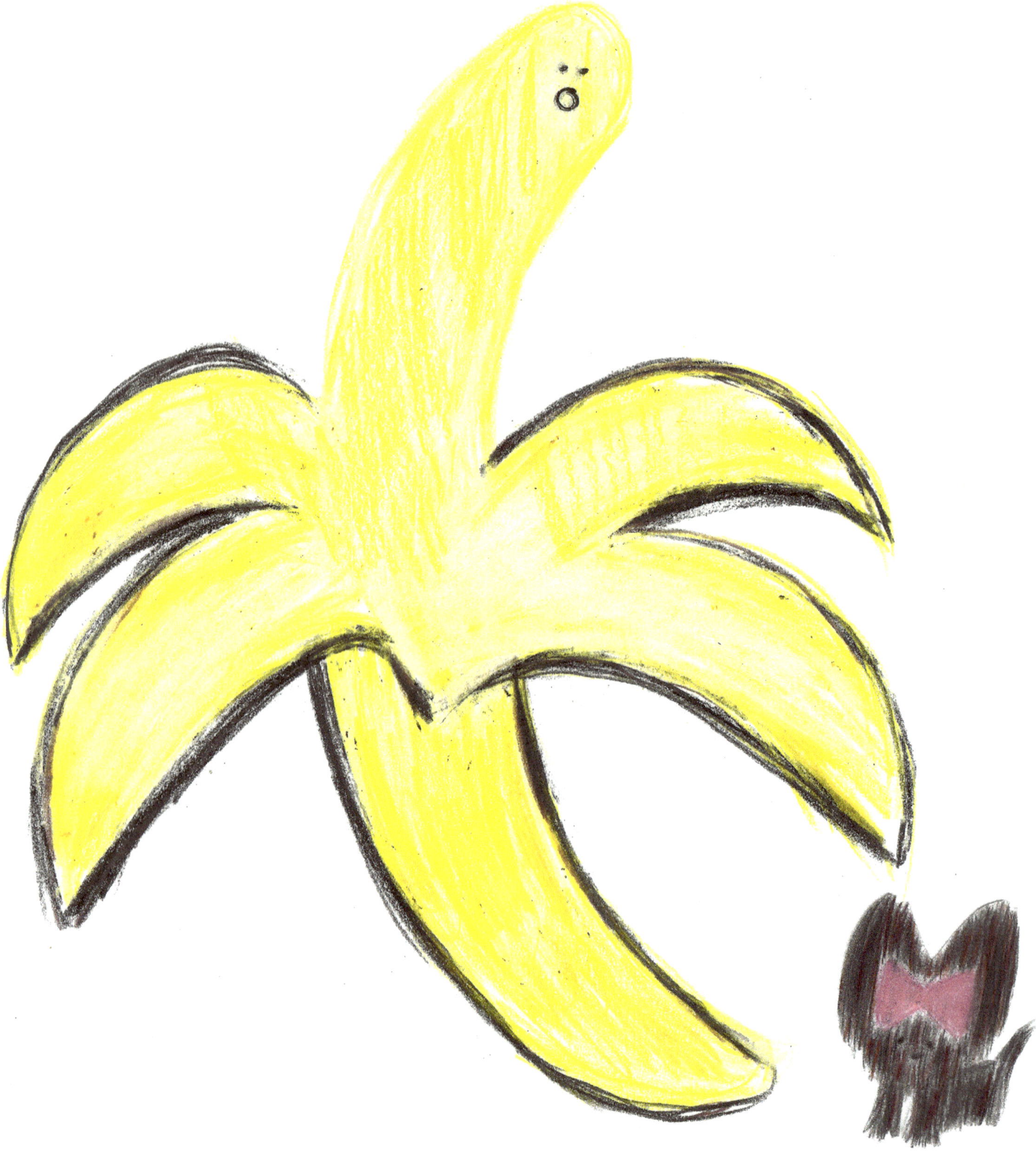

What if I only ate BANANAS every single day? Would I take the shape of a crescent and start to peel away? (*Oh no!*)

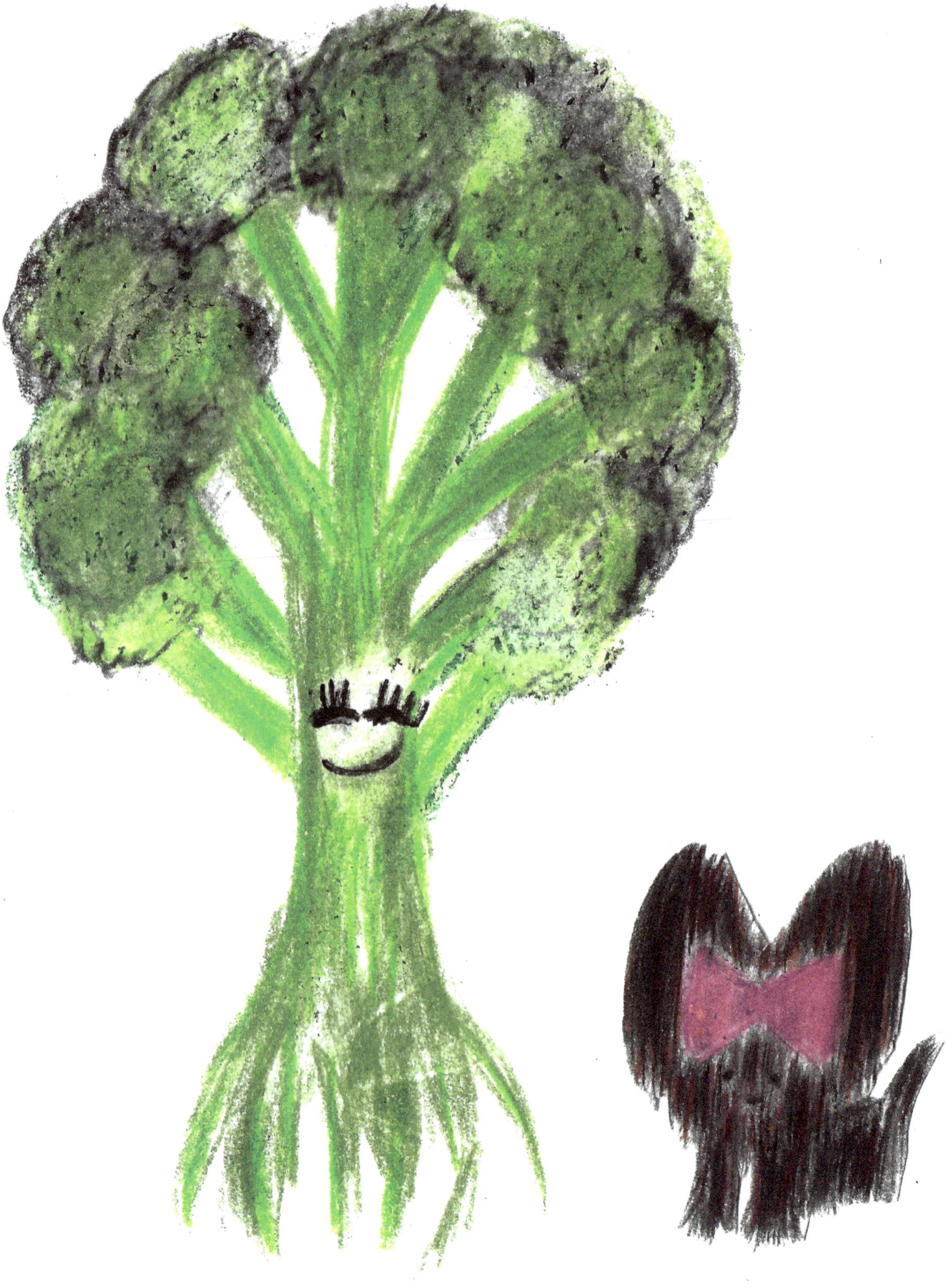

What if I only ate **BROCCOLI**? Would I look like a really tall tree?

Would my feet be planted into the ground? Would branches cover me all around?

Would I be completely shaded by green leafy sprouts? When the season changes to autumn would they all fall out?

9

What if I only ate **CANTALOUPE**? Would my head grow huge and feel rough?

Perhaps it would look like I was covered in lace or maybe it would look like I drew shapes on my face. (Ugh!)

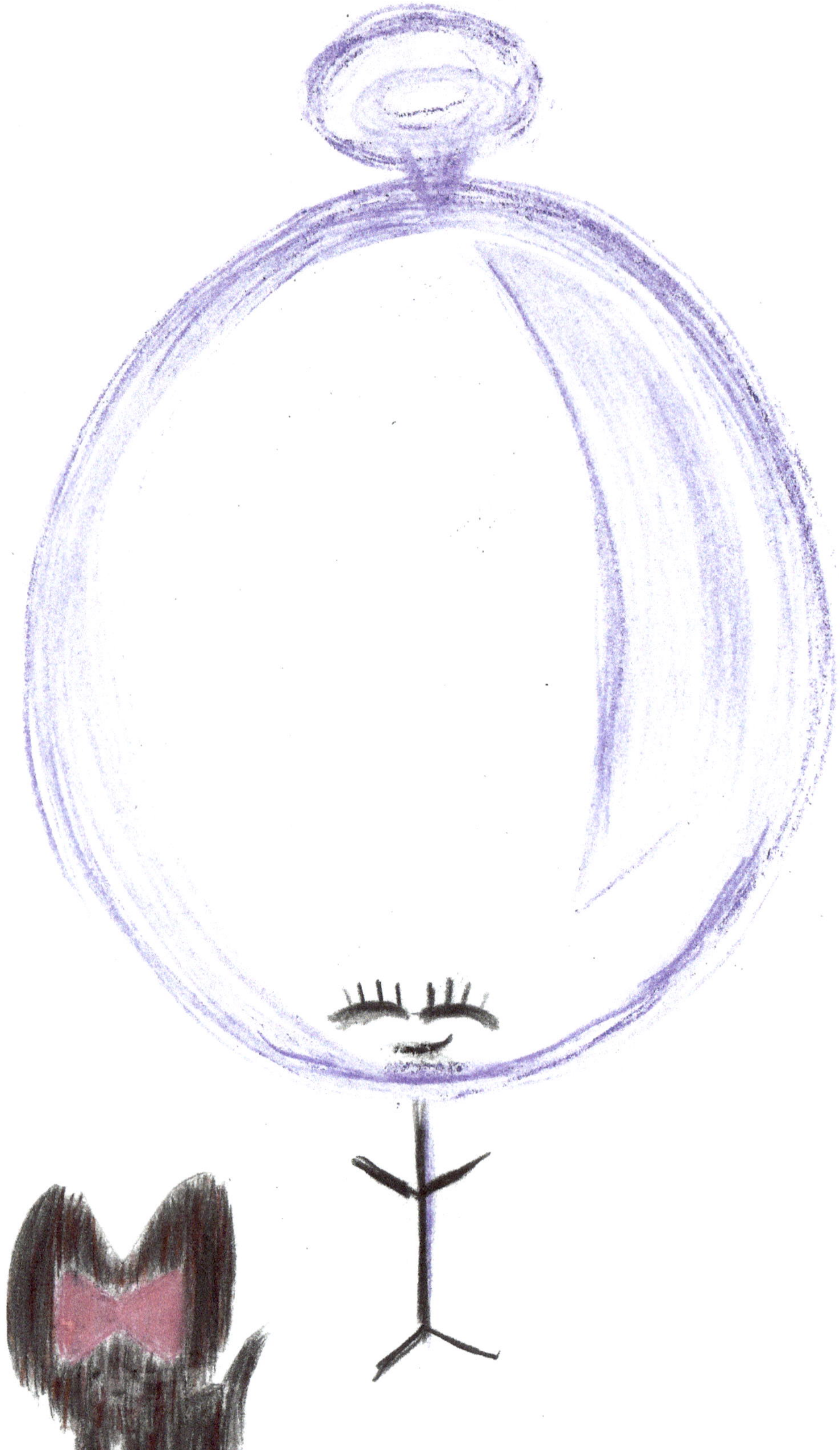

What if I only ate GRAPES? Would my color change to purple, red, or green? Would I look like an overfilled water balloon that is bursting at the seams? (Uh oh!)

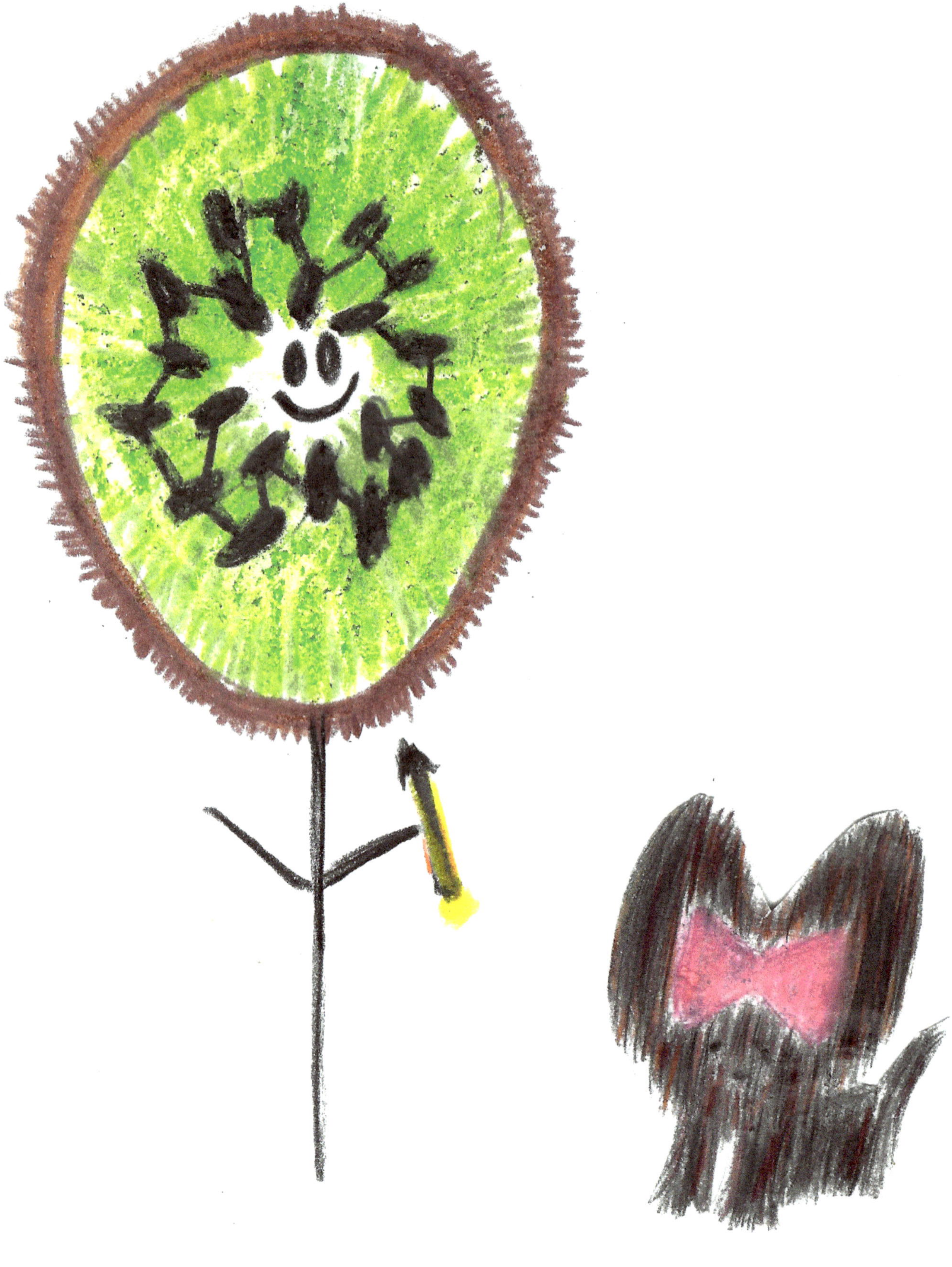

What if I only ate KIWI? Would I turn to a bright shade of green?

Would my face be outlined with black tiny spots and with a pencil I could connect the dots?

15

What if I only ate **LEMONS** for breakfast lunch and dinner? Would my face sparkle like the sun with a bright-yellow, seedy shimmer? (Fancy!!!)

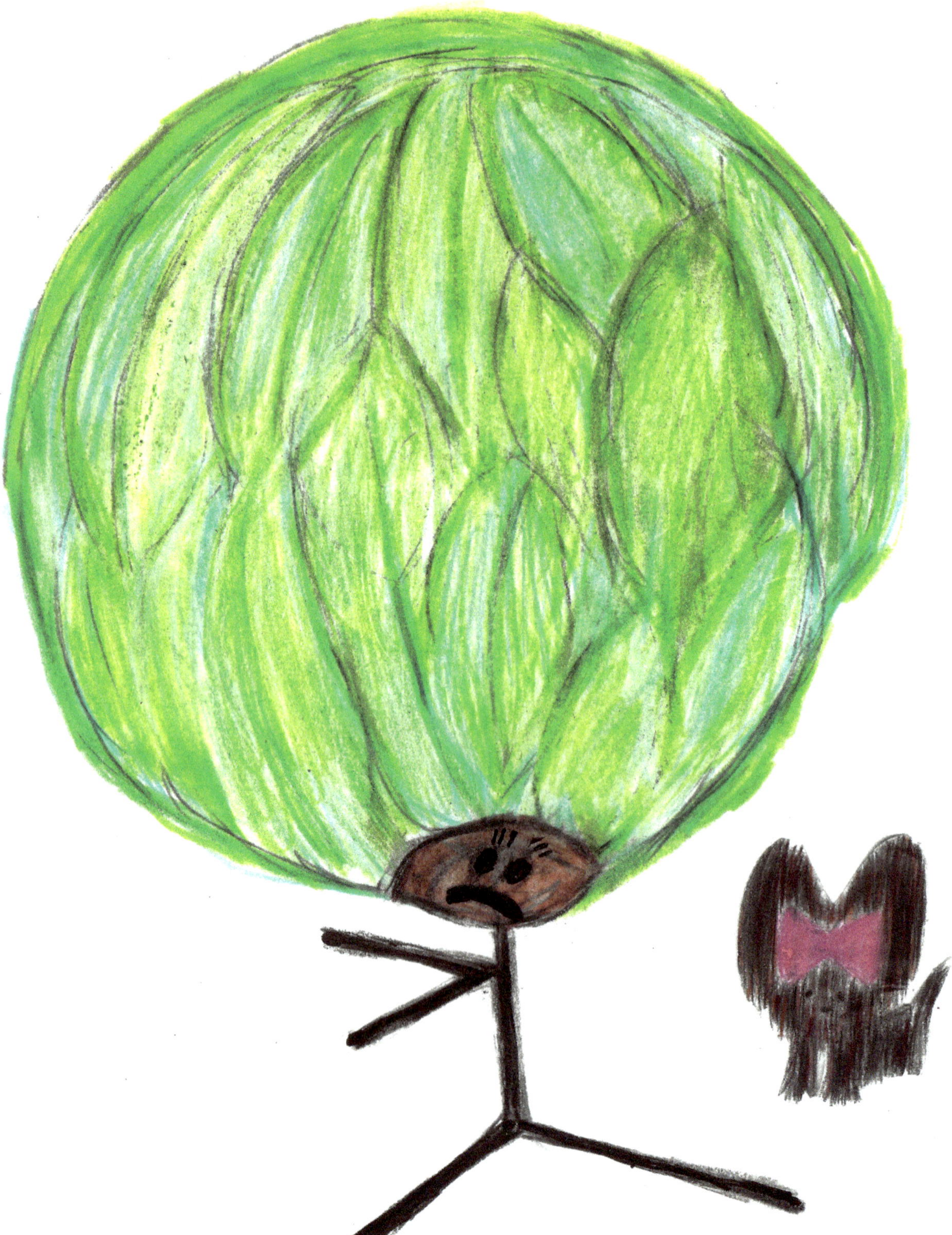

What if I only ate LETTUCE? Would I have a large layered head? Would I look like a papier-mâché project or possibly a piñata instead? (*Eeek!*)

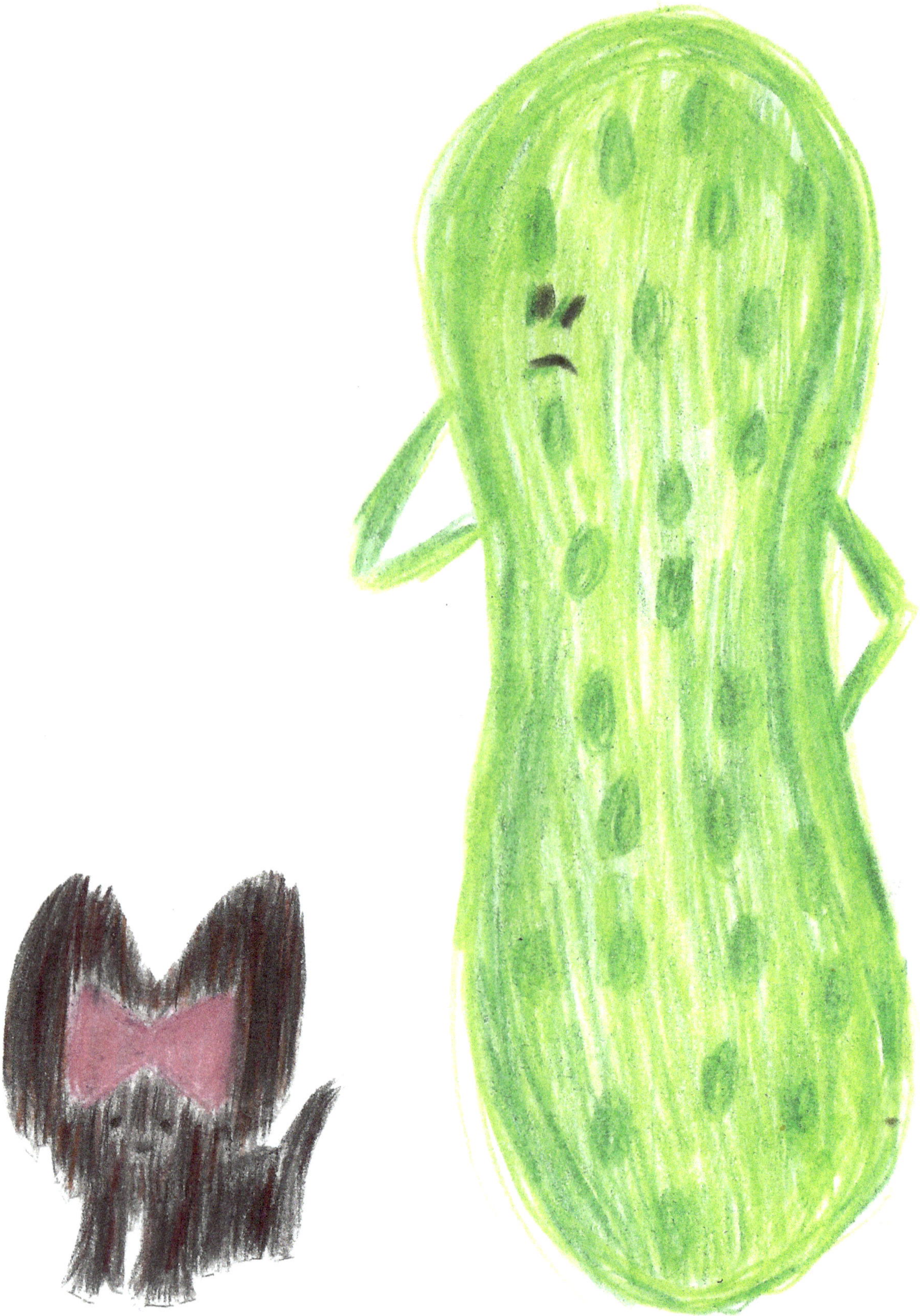

What if I only ate PICKLES? Would my skin turn bumpy and grow thick?

Would I smell kind of bad, like something went sour? (Perhaps I would need to go take a shower). I definitely wouldn't smell like a freshly picked flower! (Awe, but not that stinky!)

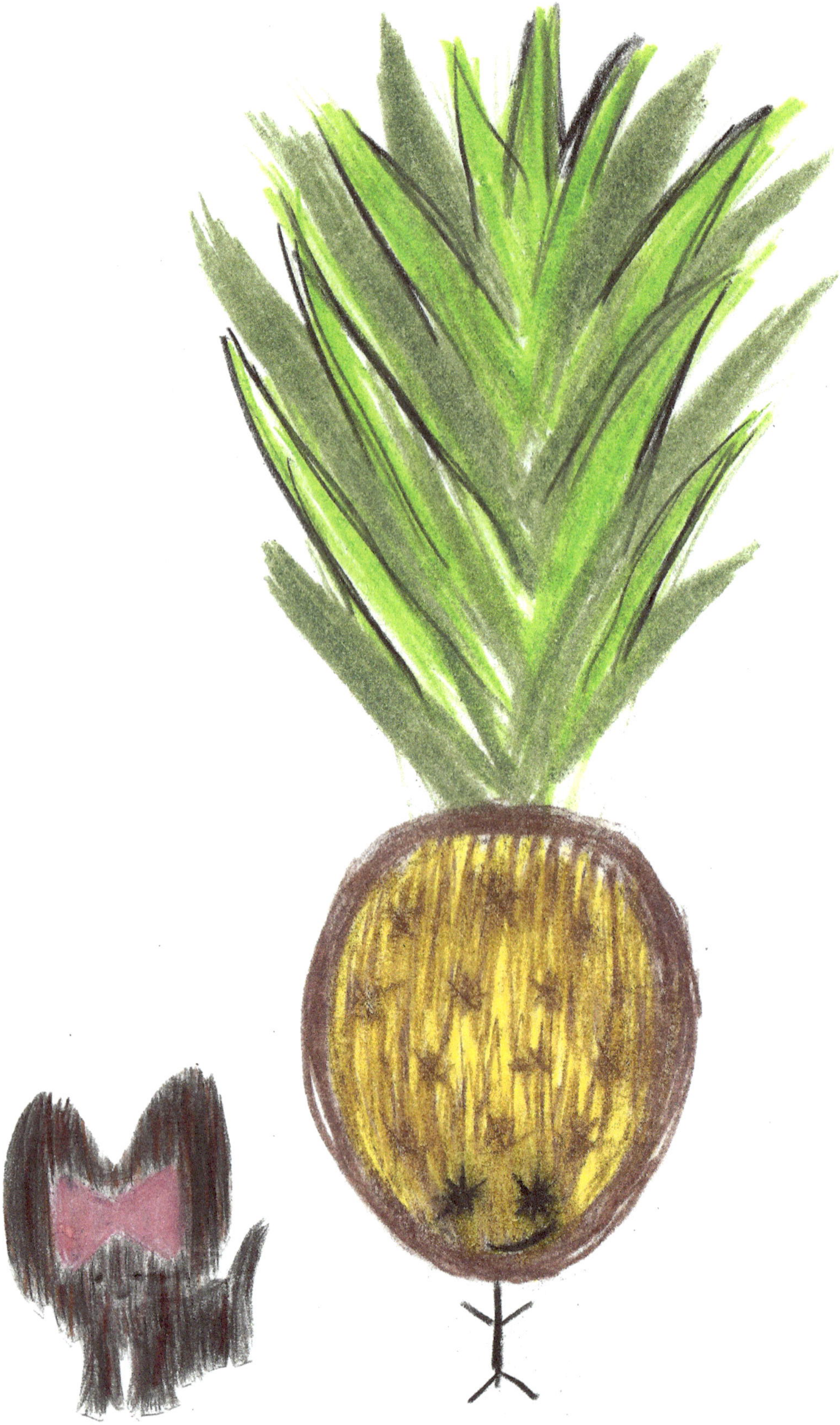

What if I only ate **PINEAPPLES**? Would a funky green Mohawk appear on my head?

Would my face look golden and be covered with spikes? I bet if you touched me you would probably yell, "*Yikes!*"

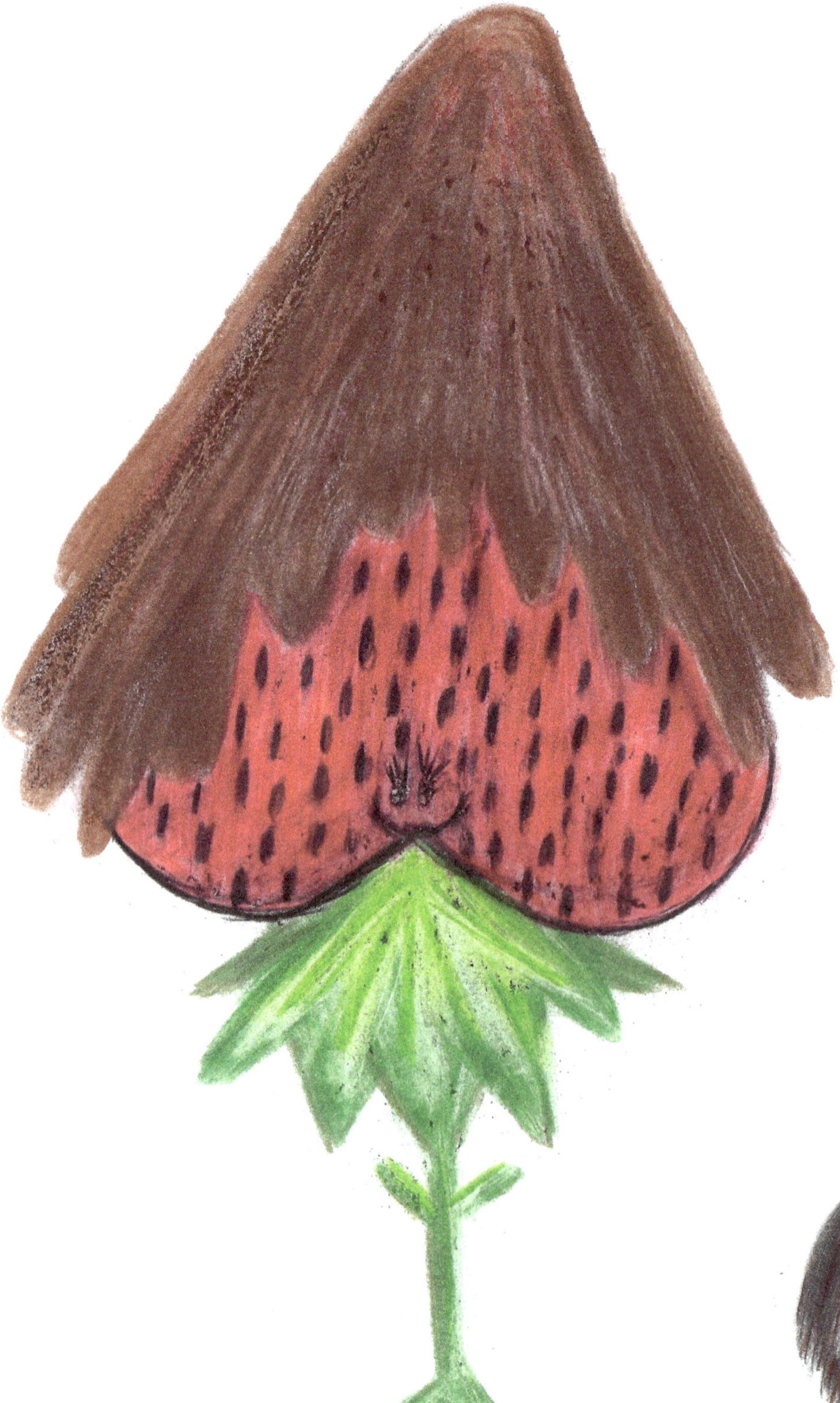

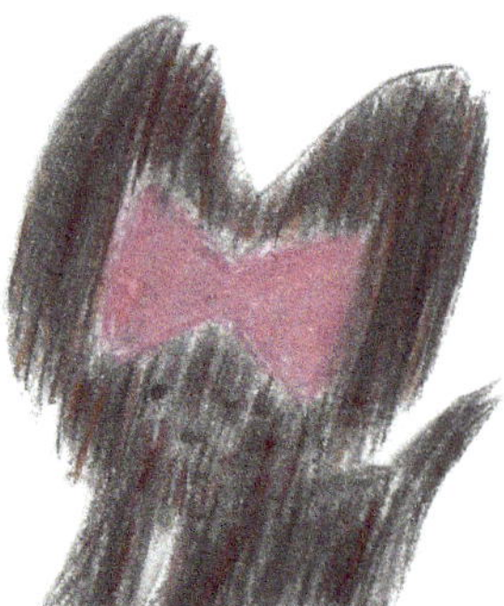

What if I only ate **STRAWBERRIES**? Would I turn a glistening shade of red? Or maybe you couldn't see my beautiful color because I was dipped in chocolate instead? (Yum!)

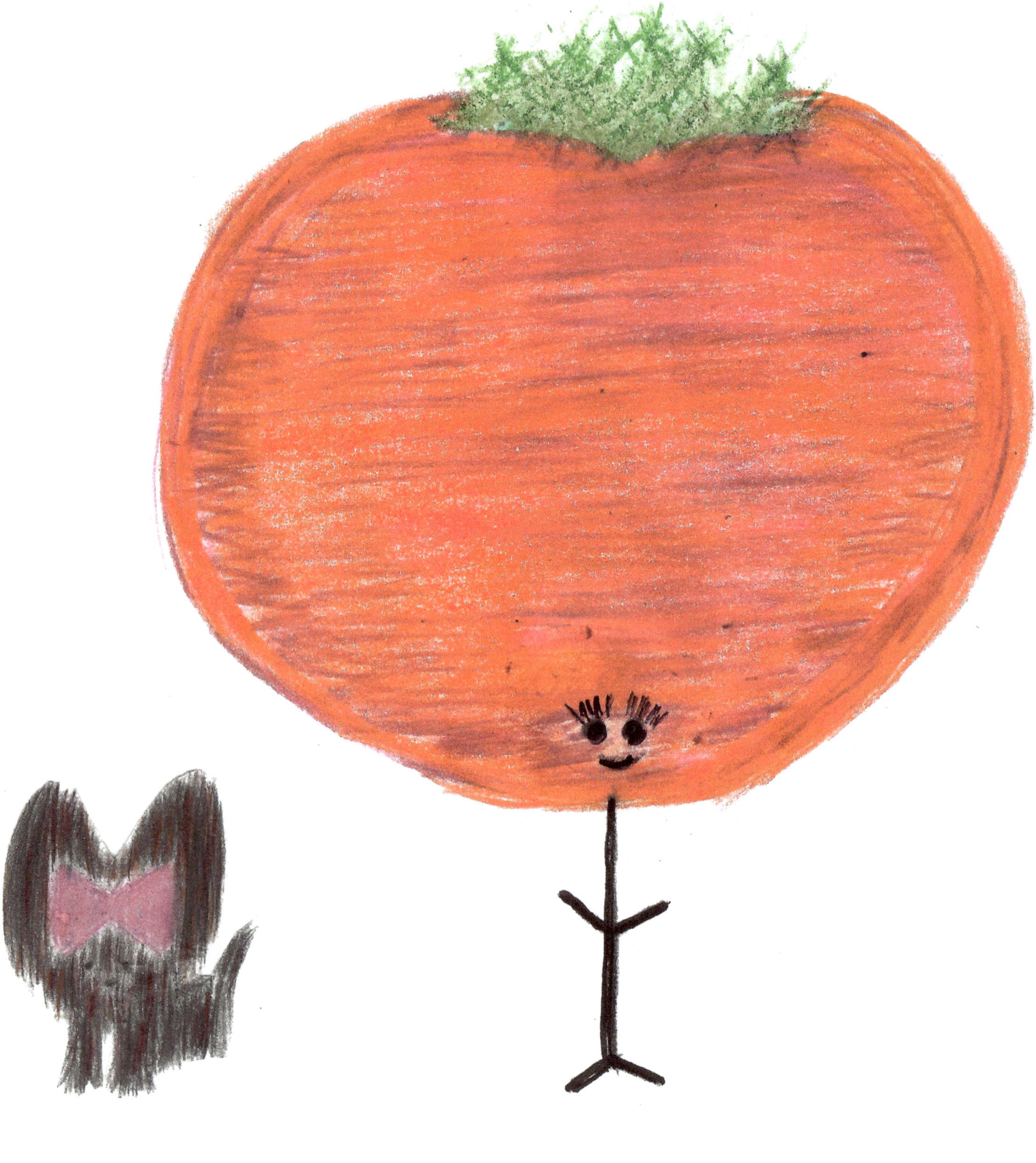

What if I only ate **TOMATOES**? Would my color change to orange or red? Would I be topped with a cluster of star-shaped leaves upon my head?

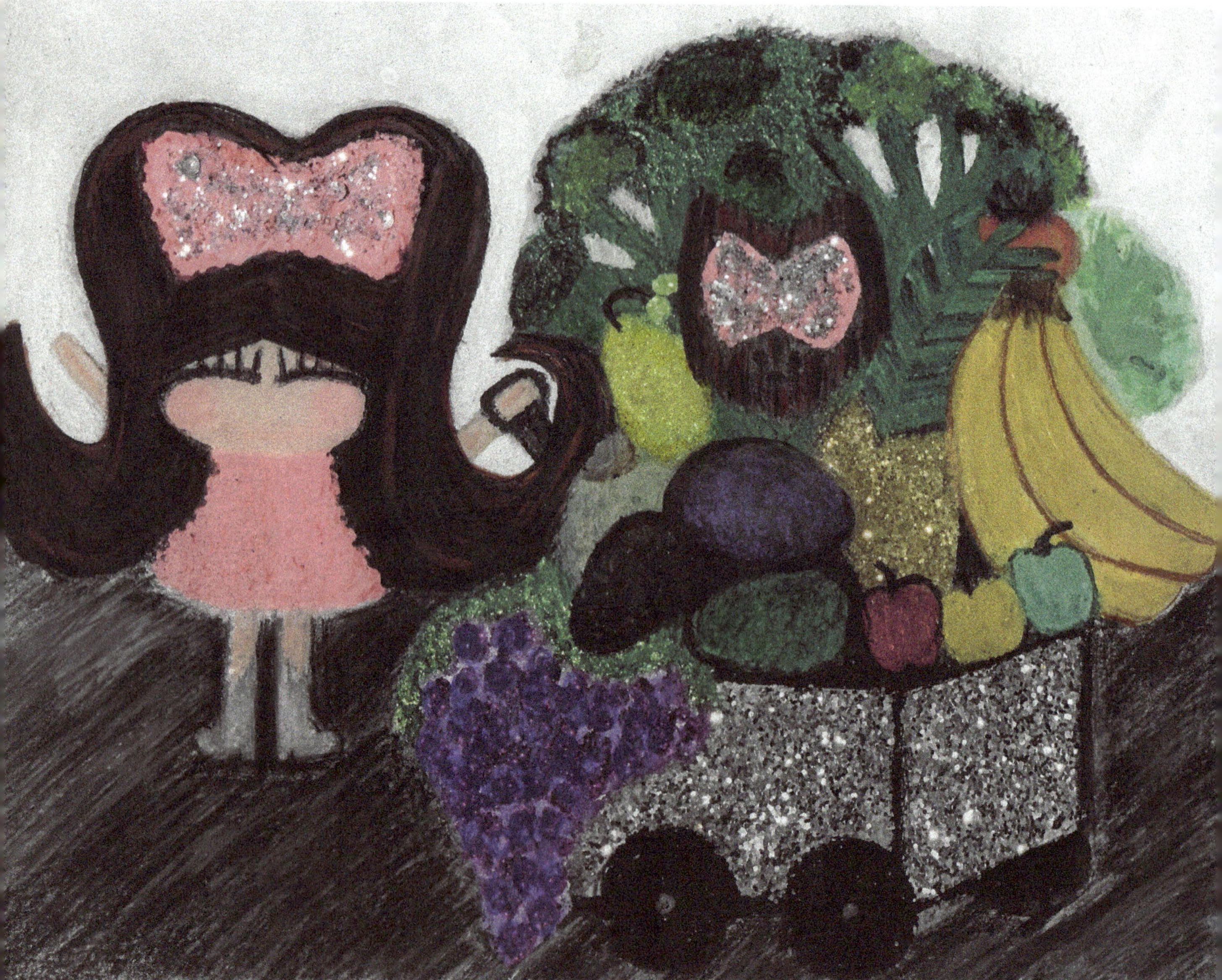

My mom and dad tell me what I should try and do, is to eat from all the food groups. A well-balanced meal three times a day is what keeps me healthy, that's what they say!

I think if I listen, I will soon see… that I love being healthy, adorable little me! (Yay!)

The End

Blessed and Thankful 😊

Dog

ABOUT THE AUTHOR

Inspired by Joey and Ava (Nicole's children) who are incredibly inquisitive and always think *big*! The concept was based on Joey's (the foodie) *huge* appetite and great love for food (especially snacks!)

Ava's *magnificent* stick-figure drawing (a true masterpiece!) really brought Sassy (aka Ava) to life. Callie, one of the family dogs (could be mistaken for a cat) was the purrrrfect bestie for Sassy!